CW00860106

Professor Curiosity Saves Christmas.

Professor Curiosity

The First Day of December.

Christmas Shopping.

The Grotto

One O'clock In The Morning.

5 days until Christmas.

Captain Christmas's Christmas Eve Eve Party.

The Doorbell.

The Journey to Toys International

The Rescue

A very special person.

A close call.

Professor Curiosity

There are a lot of things that happen in the world that only very few people know about. There are some things that even your grown-ups don't know about. A lot of grown-ups are so busy paying bills and going to work and watching the news to notice things that are happening right in front of them. If you watch very carefully you will see this happening with your grownups. Sometimes, they will be so busy staring at their phone or watching tv that they miss the wonderful things happening around them.

Grown-ups miss all sorts of things, from huge deep puddles to dogs with funny wet noses to weird smells, to amazing vehicles. They rush around so quickly through their days that they forget to look around them. Children aren't like that at all.

Children notice things. Maybe it is because children are smarter than their grown-ups or maybe it is because when you're a bit closer to the ground, you can see things differently.

If it wasn't for children so much of the world would be missed. Nobody would ever notice all the things that are going on and a lot of those things are really, very important.

Noah Fisher was one of those children who noticed everything. His Mum used to tell him that he must have eyes on the back of his head to be able to notice so many things. No matter how hard he tried bending and twisting in front of a mirror he had never been able to see if she was right. He always forgot to ask someone else to have a look for him.

Noah's Dad called him Professor Curiosity, 'You're always into everything Noah,' he would say with a big grin as he ruffled his hair, 'you're going to be a very important scientist one day, just you wait and see.'

Noah didn't want to be a scientist, he wanted to be a private detective or a spy, but he loved when his Dad said that, it made him feel warm inside. He could tell that his Dad was proud of him and that was just the best feeling ever.

Noah loved his Dad, he was his hero. Even when he was really little he would stand on the pouffé looking out the window waiting for his Dad to cycle up the street. That was Noah's favourite moment of the day, the time when all four members of his family were back in the house together listening to Dad's silly stories and watching Mum's funny dances. Noah's home was a happy place, and Noah and his little brother were both happy little boys.

Oh, I almost forgot to mention Gideon. Gideon was Noah's little brother. Gideon was very little, he was 2 years old. It took Noah a long time to get used to Gideon. When Mr and Mrs Fisher told Noah that he was going to have a little brother he wasn't very happy with the idea. He didn't want to share his Mum and Dad with anyone. Almost 3 years later Noah loved Gideon but he didn't like to play with him. Gideon never understood the rules of Noah's games and rules were very important to Noah. He did love when they would watch movies together, or when Gideon asked Noah to read him a story.

Noah was 6 and three-quarters years old. It was very important to Noah that people remembered the three quarters. He made a point of telling everyone that he was nearly 7. Being 6 was fine, but being 7 was much more grown-up, and Noah was ready for it. His birthday was in three short months and he was counting down the days. He couldn't wait for February to come.

Noah had no idea what was about to happen, nobody did, but before he would have his birthday Noah would become one of the most important people on the planet for a few days, but hardly anyone would know anything about it.

Professor Curiosity was about to save Christmas.

The First Day of December.

 I don't know what it is like where you live, but in Noah's house, the 1st December is a really important day. Noah's Mum spends almost all of November getting ready for that day. In the Fisher family home, there were lots of little rules about December 1st.

Of all the rules they had, there is one that every family in the world should follow. The Christmas tree should not be put up until 1st December at the earliest. Every year some people break this rule and put it up before December. This should be illegal. In fact, why don't you put this book down and write a letter to your MP asking them to get a law passed that stops Christmas trees being put up before December 1st. They should also ban Christmas music in shops before that date too. Last year, I saw a Christmas tree on Halloween night. That is unacceptable and we need to nip it in the bud before things get out of hand.

Sometimes Noah's Dad teased Noah's Mum about how much she cared about her 1st December traditions.

'You are basically Captain Christmas, darling. If they gave out awards for 1st December preparations you'd be the first to win one.' Noah's Dad loved giving people little nicknames like Professor Curiosity and Captain Christmas. He had hundreds of them. Some of Noah's favourites were;

Lady Letters - That was the postwoman.

The Bishop of Borehampton - The local vicar who loved to preach for about 20 minutes longer than anyone can concentrate for.

Furry Ears Freddie - This was the man next door. He had long grey hairs growing out of his ears. That is what happens to some old grown-ups. The hairs on their heads disappear and start to grow out of their noses and ears. It is very strange.

HaHaHaHarriet - Harriet ran the corner shop. She loved telling stories and always ended them with her loud and high pitched laugh. Dad did an excellent impression of her.

Of all Dad's nicknames, Noah loved Gideon's best. Mr Fisher always called Gideon Stinkpants Stinkerson. It was the truest of all the nicknames. Gideon had an amazing ability to do his business in his nappies just when the family needed to leave the house.

'Oh, come on then Stinkpants Stinkerson, let's get you changed before we are late,' Dad would say and rush up the stairs with a giggling Gideon.

When Noah got home from school on December 1st, Captain Christmas, Noah's Mum, was pacing around the kitchen with a big grin on her face. Mrs Fisher turned into a very bouncy, happy lady when she was excited. Noah loved when his Mum was like this, he could tell that she was really happy and when she was happy she was lots of fun.

'Okay, boys. Let's get started.'

She reached into a big bag on the table and started handing little packages wrapped in brown Christmas paper to Noah, Gideon and Dad.

'Oh I can't wait for you to see what I've done this year,' she said with a little bounce and a clap. 'I love Christmas so much!'

Noah already knew what was in the package. It will be pyjamas, a book and an advent calendar. That is what was always in the package, and every year Mum expected him to be surprised.

He tore the paper open slowly to reveal his Christmas pyjamas. This year they had a mouse in a red bobble hat saying, 'Merry

Christmouse' on them. Noah laughed and smiled at his Mum. 'Thanks, Mum. I love them,' he said.

'Oh there's more in there yet, Noah,' she said with another little bounce.

Noah lifted out the book and Advent calendar. A Christmas Carol (retold for children) and a Chocolate Elves and Reindeer calendar.

'Open the door Noah, open the door,' said Mum as if she was going to burst.

Noah sat on the floor and after a little bit of a struggle, he eventually managed to open the little cardboard door. Out popped a little chocolate elf head. He took a little nibble of it and the wonderful creamy chocolate melted on his tongue.

'So good, Mum. Thank you!' he said smiling at his Mum. Noah's Mum was very specific with the Advent calendars she bought her boys. She insisted on buying a certain brand because, in her words, the other brand tastes like soap. This little elf head definitely didn't taste like soap.

Every morning, just before breakfast, the Fishers would stand in a row in front of the fireplace and open that day's door of their calendar. They'd each eat their chocolate together and make various noises that all meant 'yummy!'

On the 19th December, just five days before the big day, and the first day of the school holidays, Noah joined Mum, Dad and little Gideon in front of the fire and opened door number 19. He looked inside for an elf or a reindeer but to his surprise, there wasn't chocolate in there at all. Instead, there was a little square piece of folded Christmas wrapping paper. He looked at his Mum who for the first time that morning had stopped jigging around.

'Well, I'll take it back to the shop and get a new one, something has gone wrong with this one. Darling, do we still have the receipt? I will get you a new one, Noah, don't you worry. Here, have my chocolate.'

Noah put the little piece of paper in his pocket and hugged Captain Christmas.

'Thanks, Mum. You're the best.'

A little later on that day, Noah was in his room when he remembered about the piece of paper. He lifted it out of his pocket and looked at it thinking about how strange it was that a little piece of paper like that would end up behind that door.

He unfolded the paper and to his surprise, he noticed that it had a little message written on it. As he read the note every little bit of curiosity in Professor Curiosity's young mind was woken up. He read it over and over again wondering if it said what he thought it said. If it did, Noah's life just got very interesting indeed.

The note said;

"If you are reading this we need help. Please look out for the signs. Christmas depends on it.

Elmo V. Mistletoe."

After dinner, Noah was on the sofa in his new pyjamas reading the note. He wasn't sure what to think. Whoever wrote that note, Elmo V Mistletoe seemed to be in a lot of trouble and Noah is the one who found it so he had to help if he could. The problem was, what did they need help with and what sort of trouble were they in? Noah needed to get answers but he had no idea where to start.

'What's that, Noah?' Dad asked, staring at the note.

'Umm. Nothing, Dad,' said Noah. He didn't know why he lied but he just didn't think it was the right time to tell anyone about the note. Something as important as this should be handled with great care. Once he knew more about what was going on Noah would tell his Dad all about it.

'Well, you and that nothing need to get upstairs for bed. Don't forget to brush your teeth. Mum's bought new Christmas toothpaste. The tube plays a carol every time you squeeze it. Captain Christmas strikes again!'

'Okay, Dad, I love you. Night night. Night, Mum,' said Noah and gave them both a squeeze and a kiss.

As Noah put his head down on the pillow, he knew he wouldn't get to sleep quickly because he had important thinking to do about the note.

Christmas Shopping.

Noah woke up the next day to the sound of Gideon banging on his bedroom door. Gideon couldn't reach the door handle yet so this was his way of getting his parents' attention.

Noah woke up and realised that the note was still lying next to him on the pillow. He didn't remember falling asleep, but he did remember that he had decided that the best thing to do was to spend the day with his eyes peeled for other clues as to what the note might mean. This was his big chance to do some real detective work.

If he didn't see anything, then maybe the note was just someone's idea of a joke, though he didn't see how it was funny. However, he was determined that if there was something to see, he was not going to miss it.

Noah made a little box out of some plastic blocks he had in his room and placed the note inside. He pushed it right under his bed as far as he could reach. This seemed to be the safest place to hide the note. Nobody would ever look under there.

'Breakfaaaaast,' came a shout from downstairs, and so began day two of the big adventure that Noah didn't even know he was on yet.

An hour after breakfast, Noah and Gideon were being bundled up in their coats and hats to go to town for some Christmas shopping. Noah didn't enjoy shopping. It wasn't just because sometimes the lights were too bright and the sounds were too loud, but most of all, it was because shopping was boring.

Noah always felt that on the days when the family went to the shops, he spent too much time watching his Mum smelling candles and his Dad flicking through books that he never bought. This time was different. Noah felt that he could use that waiting around time to look for clues but not just that, his Dad had promised him a chocolate coin from a coffee shop. Christmas is great for getting extra chocolate.

'Oh, I forgot something,' said Noah running up the stairs.

'You've only one shoe on, get back here,' Dad said with a voice that was a little louder than normal. Dad always got frustrated when the family were leaving the house. It seemed like Dad got frustrated about very strange little things.

'Oh, I'll be right back,' Noah called from his room as he lifted his little orange notebook and pencil from his desk and slipped them into his coat pocket. If Noah was going to find some clues, he needed to make sure that he kept a very good record of what those clues were. That's what good detectives do, and that is what Noah was going to do too.

The town was really busy. This was another thing that made Dad huff and puff a little but everyone was having a good day. There was lots of Christmas music playing and the shops were full of things to look at and hundreds of good ideas as to what children might want for Christmas.

By lunchtime, Noah hadn't noticed anything strange at all. Well, that's not exactly true. There was a woman in the middle of town who was dressed as a reindeer that was pretending to be a statue. The thing was, she didn't look much like a reindeer and if Noah looked hard enough he could see her moving. She didn't like it when Noah pointed this out to her.

People kept giving her money anyway which confused Noah a lot; grownups are weird sometimes. As he was finishing his cheese sandwich in Mrs Barker's Coffee House, Noah noticed something happening outside the window in the street below.

A man and a woman wearing matching uniforms were wrapping yellow tape around the Santa's Grotto and sticking signs on the windows and door of the little shed that Santa sat in every day.

Every year, from 1st December until 23rd December, Santa's Grotto was open in the middle of town. Santa would sit in his little shed with his two elves. Children, and even some adults, would go in and get a chance to tell Santa what they wanted for Christmas that year and Santa would give every child a little Selection Box of chocolate bars (more chocolate!) and their grown-ups would try to get a photo of them smiling. Gideon cried a lot last year. Noah thinks he was scared of the elves.

Noah lifted his notebook out of his pocket and wrote down what he could see. Was this another clue? From up in the window of Mrs Barker's Coffee House he couldn't read the signs or the writing on the tape but he would make sure he would get closer so that he could find out more.

'Santa's Grotto. Something weird. Check later,' Noah wrote in his book and slipped it back into his coat. He then took the first bite of his chocolate coin. It was delicious.

'I love Christmas,' said Noah's Mum.
'We know!' came the reply from Noah and his Dad at the same time.

The Grotto

 A few minutes later they were back outside in the cold and Noah was trying to think of a way that he could get to the Grotto to take a look. Just at that moment, he had a stroke of luck.

'Oh I love this song,' said his very excited Mum, 'let's go listen, boys. With that, she started walking towards the square where the Grotto was. In the middle of the square, just in front of the Grotto was a man in one of those posh suits that famous people wear to parties. He had a hat on that looked like a Turkey with a red bow around it.

He was singing that Christmas song about chestnuts and fires and Jack Frost. Noah didn't like that song, but on this occasion, he was really glad to hear it because his Mum had led the family to a spot right in front of the Grotto They were 2 metres away from the turkey-hatted singer and 3 metres away from the signs

that Noah needed to read.

The turkey-hatted singer must be very popular with grownups because there was a big group of people singing along and smiling. They kept walking over to him and giving him money which they put in a stocking hanging from his microphone stand.

Maybe it was for a new hat. The turkey one didn't match his suit at all.

Noah was so close to the sign but the problem was, the crowd was so tightly packed that he couldn't see them read what they said. He needed to get closer.

At that moment, Noah had another stroke of luck, his Dad let go of his hand so that he could record the singing on his phone. Grownups have a habit of not watching the world through their eyes but watching it through their phones. Noah noticed this a lot. If anything good or strange or exciting was happening grown-ups were always taking photos or videos on their phones. His Dad took a lot of photos of cups of coffee that as far as Noah could see all looked the same. Today, however, Noah was really glad that his Dad wanted to take a video of the singer.

It gave him just long enough to sneak away to read the sign.

Now, if you are reading this, you should know that what Noah did is not a good thing to do at all. Noah got into a little bit of trouble that day for doing it. Never sneak away from your grown-up, not even if it is to read a sign on Santa's Grotto. Sometimes Noah made good choices, sometimes he made choices that weren't so good. This was one of those not so good choices. This time nothing bad happened but it could have. Always stay close.

Noah took his chance and dropped to his hands and knees and crawled through the legs of the crowd so that he could get a little closer to the grotto. When he got to about 1 metre away he stood up to realise that he couldn't get any closer. The path was blocked by yellow tape that said in big black letters, 'DO NOT ENTER.' Luckily, he was close enough to read the sign. He grabbed his notebook and pencil and copied down the words.

'Due to unforeseen circumstances, Santa's Grotto is not operating until further notice.'

'Pssst.'

Noah wrote the last word in his notebook and looked up to see what that noise was.

'Pssst. Over here.' Noah still couldn't see where the voice was coming from.

'The Grotto door. Over here.' Noah looked at the door and could see the face of one of the elves, the one that Gideon was afraid of, looking out through a little opening in the wood.

'Did you get the note?' asked the elf, 'the one in the calendar.'

Noah nodded to say yes.

'Good. I sent it. We need help. We need your help, Noah. We will come and see you later at your house. Be in the living room at 1 am. Don't be late,' then the face disappeared as quickly as it had appeared.

'NOAH! What are you doing! You can't run away like that. Not in a crowd like this. Anything could happen. That was silly,' Noah's Mum was not happy at all.

'Sorry Mum. It's just that…' Noah started to reply.

'It's just nothing, Noah. Never walk away like that. You're much too precious to lose.'

'Okay, Mum. I won't do it again,' Noah said quietly. He looked up at his Dad who winked at him shaking his head.

'Professor Curiosity. What will we do with you, eh?' He said with a smile, 'Right, let's get home. It's pizza night at the Fishers'.'

One O'clock In The Morning.

 As soon as Noah got home he ran upstairs to write down everything he could remember the elf had said down. He tore out one page from his little orange book and wrote in big letters, '1 a.m. Living Room.' He reached up and gently peeled back the corner of his Apollo 11 poster and took a little bit of sticky tack out and stuck the page to the wall beside his bed.

He couldn't forget that information and this is what he saw Mum do with notes on the fridge when she needed to remember things. In Noah's house, his Mum remembered things that his Dad would forget. His Dad claimed to have a brilliant memory but every week he forgot to take the recycling out. This always led to a frantic panic on Tuesday mornings as Dad ran into the street in his slippers just as the recycling truck pulled into their street.

The latest Noah had ever been awake before was 9.30 pm and that was when they got stuck in traffic on the drive home from a holiday in Scotland. That drive took hours and hours. As far as Noah could tell Scotland was the furthest place anyone would ever need to travel. If travelling took that long, he was happy to stay at home. He remembers being sleepy and tired at 9.30 pm. How was he ever going to stay awake until 1 am? He needed something to wake him up.

'I know!' he said out loud and ran downstairs to the toy drawers in the living room. A few weeks ago Noah had found a stopwatch in a charity shop and his Mum had bought it for him. Of all the things in the world, Noah loved numbers the most. He loved how numbers were always the same. Words could sometimes be confusing, they meant different things and sometimes words said in a different way meant the opposite of what he thought they meant. Numbers didn't do that. Noah's Dad always told people that Noah's first words were one, two and three and as a baby, his favourite toy was a calculator.

The stopwatch was great. Noah used to sit on his bed and watch the numbers go up and he would try to press the button to get it to stop as close to 7 seconds as he could. His record was 7.05 seconds. One day he would get the bullseye! The other thing Noah had remembered, that had caused him to rush to get his stopwatch, is that it also had an alarm on it that beeped at the right time.

Noah grabbed his stopwatch.

'What are you in such a rush for Noah?' asked Mum.

'Just timing things Mum,' Noah replied as he ran out of the room.

'You forgot to close the door!' Mum shouted.

'Sorry!' said Noah bouncing back and pulling the door closed.

Noah ran back to his room and sat on his bed. He pushed the buttons on the top of his stopwatch until he was at the alarm. He set the alarm to go off as 12.55 am. That gave him enough time to sneak downstairs and get to the living room in time for the elves.

He put his notebook and his stopwatch under his pillow and went downstairs for dinner.

Everything was ready. Pizza night was his favourite.

BEEP. BEEP. BEEP. BEEP.

Noah sat up in bed. At the moment between asleep and awake, he had forgotten all about the alarm. He had been dreaming about a huge lorry full of chocolate coins reversing into his driveway. He hadn't even got the chance to eat one before the alarm had woken him up.

'Oh! It's the alarm,' Noah whispered to himself as he thrust his hand under the pillow to stop the beeping. He listened carefully to see if anyone had heard the beeps but he couldn't hear anything except snoring from Mum and Dad's room. He reached under the bed and lifted his little torch that he kept there for reading in secret after his parents had turned the lights off, grabbed his notebook and quietly got out of bed.

Why is it that when someone is trying to be quiet at night that the only floorboards they put their feet on are the ones that creak the loudest? Noah's first step across his room let out a huge creak.

'Shhh!' Noah said to the floor and then laughed at how silly it was to speak to a piece of wood. He slowly opened his door and made his way downstairs, his little torch lighting up every footstep.

He opened the living room door and stepped inside. It was still nice and warm in the living room. The last embers of the fire were in the wood burning stove. He sat close to the warmth and waited. He could feel his heart beating in his chest. This was exciting. He was as close to being a Private Detective as he ever had been and he didn't even need to leave his house.

'Psst. Wake up.'
Noah sat up and looked into the face of the elf. He didn't remember falling asleep, maybe it was the warmth of the fire. He shone his torch onto the clock on the wall. It said that it was one minute past one.

'I must have fallen asleep for a minute or two there. Sorry Mr, umm. Mr I don't know your name,' said Noah sleepily.

In reality, Noah had fallen asleep for an hour and 15 minutes. You see, what he forgot to do was check that the time on his stopwatch, matched the actual time. Fortunately, his stopwatch was running fast. If it had been slow, he'd have missed the elf altogether. Instead, he got to have a nap on the carpet.

'You do know my name, Noah. I wrote it on the letter,' said the elf in that strange voice that elves speak in that is sort of high pitched and like they are singing a song.

'OH YES!' Noah said pointing his finger in the air. Noah always did this when he had a good idea. His Dad called it his light bulb finger. Noah didn't know why. He grabbed his notebook and found the first page.

'Are you Elmo V. Mistletoe?'
'I am. Very good work Noah. I'm glad you managed to get to us earlier. We have a big problem,' said Elmo. This time, his voice wasn't like a sing-song at all. He seemed worried and sad.

Noah, having to ignore the weirdness of the fact that he was talking to an elf in his living room, took out his pencil and turned to a fresh page.

'Tell me everything, Elmo. What's going on and why did you choose me to help?' Noah asked.

'Noah, we have a big problem. I knew we couldn't go to a grownup, they are always too busy looking into their phones, we knew a child had to help us. Children notice things that adults don't and we know that of all the children you notice more than most. You were the one to help us.' the elf said, his voice calming a little.

'Three days ago we were setting up The Grotto in town with Santa. Elsie and I, she is the other elf, went to get Gingerbread Lattes from Mrs Barker's and when we arrived back Santa was gone. He had disappeared. At first, we thought maybe he had gone to get something but after an hour or two we started to worry. That is when I noticed this note on the floor.'

Elmo handed Noah a piece of paper with big black letters written on it.

'Don't look for him. You will never find him,' it read.

'Who wrote this?' asked Noah.

'Well,' said Elmo, 'At first we had no idea but then Elsie found this, underneath one of the boxes in the Grotto.' Elmo handed Noah a crumpled up card, like the ones people carry in their wallets with their address on them.

Elmo continued, 'We immediately knew it was a clue and worked out exactly what had happened. It is worse than we could ever believe.'

Elmo was starting to look worded, his little forehead was getting very wrinkly underneath his green hat and his pointed ears looked like they were drooping down. Noah looked at the card and read it out loud.

'Mr Nigel Grim, Head of Security. Toys International Inc. I don't understand what this means, Elmo. Who is Nigel and who are Toys International Inc.?' Noah asked with a yawn. It was now half-past one, Noah was normally fast asleep.

'Noah, you just stay awake. Listen very carefully and write this down. Toys International Inc. is Santa's biggest rival. About 15 years ago a woman called Meredith Bleak realised that there was a lot of money to be made from Christmas.

For hundreds of years Santa and been making and delivering toys to children for free but, as some grown-ups often do, Meredith Bleak wanted to turn something that was giving joy to every child in the world into a money-making scheme. They've done it with almost everything, water, forests fruit; soon they'll be selling air.

Well, for years she has been trying to get Santa out of the way so that she could sell toys to all the children in the world. She thinks that if she can get rid of Santa and step in with an offer to replace his free toys with her horrible factories toys that she can become a bazillionaire.'

'Bazillion isn't a real number, Elmo,' Noah interrupted.

'Well, super-rich then!' the elf continued, 'we are sure that Meredith and her henchmen have got Santa and we need you to help us get her back.'

'Why me? Why not a grown-up?' asked Noah through a yawn.

'They never notice anything. You notice everything. It's like you have eyes on …'

'Back of my head. I know. Mum says that. Okay, I'll help you, but I have no idea how. How long do we have?' Noah's mind was racing but he couldn't come up with any ideas.

'Well, it's Christmas in 5 days. You'll think of something. If you need to tell me anything, Noah, stick a note outside your window. I'll be checking. Okay, I better go and you better go to bed,' and just like that he was gone and Noah quietly crept upstairs and back to bed.

5 days until Christmas.

'Why are you tired this morning,' asked Dad, 'you've been yawning ever since you woke up. You didn't go on some kind of adventure when we're all asleep, did you? Or were you up all night doing some wild science experiments, Professor Curiosity?'

Noah laughed. Dad was almost always being silly and Noah loved that about him.

'No adventures or experiments, Dad. think I just didn't sleep well maybe. I'll get to bed early tonight. Can I just curl up on the sofa and watch some tv for a bit, please?'

Noah's Dad nodded and turned on the tv and flicked to the children's channel. To everyone's surprise, instead of dog superheroes or taking cars being on, it was The Prime Minister, Eleanor Stiles, with a Christmas Pudding hat on her head. Why do so many people wear silly hats at Christmas?

When you think of a Prime Minister or a politician you might think about a person with a grey suit and grey hair and a very boring voice but Eleanor Stiles was not like that at all. Eleanor Stiles was, just like her name suggests, a style icon. She had a lot of fans, and perhaps her biggest fan of all was Noah's Mum.

'Ellie's on the telly again, Love,' Dad called through to the kitchen where Mum was making her fourth cup of tea of the day.

'Oh good,' Mum said as she skipped into the lounge, dribbling tea as she did. 'Did you know she was the youngest ever Queen's Counsel (a very important lawyer) and the first black Prime Minister, Noah? Oh, spilt I love her suit! Turn it up. I can't hear what she's saying,' Mum said looking around the room as if the noise was coming from the boys.

Dad turned the volume up and looked at Noah. Mum was the only one talking. She got so excited about Eleanor.

'So, this is your chance to have your Christmas card displayed at Number 10 Downing Street. Design your best card and send it to me. 100 lucky children can have their cards displayed and will get a card back from me.'

Eleanor was a captivating woman. It was clear to everyone that she knew exactly what to do in every situation. Noah's Mum always said that Eleanor Stiles would be known as the smartest Prime Minister ever.

'You should make one Noah! You could get a card from Eleanor. Oh, how exciting! I'll get the craft box,' said Mum rushing out of the room almost slipping on the tea she'd spilled earlier.

Noah wasn't very keen on making a card. He was much more interested in numbers and science than he was in art. It felt like a waste of time when he should be focussed on trying to save Santa.

A few moments later, Noah was sticking shiny green and red triangles onto the front of a piece of the folded card. He was covered in glitter and had somehow managed to get glue in his hair.

'You have an amazing ability to spread craft materials across your face, Noah,' said Dad, 'maybe we should call you Professor Sparkles from now on!'

Just then Noah had an idea, a really a good idea. Noah didn't know what to do to help Santa but he was sure that Eleanor Stiles would. She always seemed to know what to do and he had a small chance of getting a message to her.

Noah has to make this card look as amazing as possible. He started to concentrate more on his work. I don't know about you, but when Noah was concentrating hard he would stick his tongue out. He wasn't sure why he did that but something about his tongue being out helped him focus and on this occasion, it worked.

'Wow, Noah, I think that's your best work ever,' said Mum with a big grin, 'I think maybe you want to impress Eleanor just as much as I do, I mean, sorry, well, that's a great card is what I mean.'

'Thanks, Mum,' Noah smiled back, 'can I write the message myself, I don't want anyone else to see.'

'Of course, buddy. It's your card,' Mum replied. Deep down she wanted to be writing the card but she knew she should leave this one to Noah.

'Dear Prime Minister,
My name is Noah Fisher and I am six and three quarters and I need your help. There's not enough room in this card to explain but I have found out that Santa has been

kidnapped and needs to be rescued. Can you help? You will know what to do.

I live at 5 East Green Avenue, York if you can help please come there.

Yours faithfully,
Noah Fisher, Schoolboy.'

Noah didn't know how to end a letter but he'd seen that written on one that his Dad had received from the bank, so he went with that. Noah folded the card and put it in the envelope.

'Please work!' he said to the envelope, 'this is our best chance of saving Santa.'

With that, he walked downstairs and handed the envelope to his Mum. She opened her wallet, pulled out a stamp and stuck it on the top right-hand corner. Mum's always have stamps, they are always ready to send a birthday card with a moment's notice.

'Can I go post it now, Mum?' Noah asked, 'it feels really important.'

'See if your Dad will walk you to the post box. I don't think he's doing anything right now,' Mum replied, 'I'm going to make some tasty, Christmas shortbread. I'll get some Christmas playing. Oh, I love Christmas.'

'I know you do, Mum,' Noah said as he set off to find his Dad.

A few minutes later Noah closed his eyes and posted the card.

'Please work,' he whispered one more time, 'please work.'

'Shall we go home for a some chocolate, Professor?' asked Dad, 'race you!'

Captain Christmas's Christmas Eve Eve Party.

The following day was a big day in the Fisher house. Captain Christmas, Noah's Mum, was hosting her, Christmas Eve Eve Party. Every year on the day before Christmas Eve all of Noah's family came round for party games, mince pies and the exchanging Christmas presents.

Mrs Fisher started her preparations early in the morning. By the time Noah, Gideon and Dad got up the house smelled of wonderful baking and mulled wine. There were Christmas carols playing on the smart speaker in the kitchen and the tree lights were sparkling.

Breakfast on Christmas Eve Eve was always the same; Dad's Christmas Pancakes. Now, I'm going to let you in on a secret that not many people know. Make sure you don't tell anyone this, but Dad's Christmas pancakes were the same as any other pancakes you might have had. There was nothing Christmassy about them except that Dad made them on the 23rd December but Dad insisted that they were special and everyone seemed to go along with it. Noah loved pancakes, especially with banana and chocolate spread.

'I'll take the boys to the park today, Love, to give you some space. I'll pick up the wine, do you need anything?' Dad asked Mum between gulps of coffee.

'I haven't managed to get my traditional Christmas treat yet, so a bottle of that would be great.' Mum winked at Dad.

Every year Mum treated herself to something called Irish Cream. Apart from Irish Cream all Mum ever seemed to drink was tea or water, but at Christmas, she would always have this special drink. Noah couldn't understand why she liked it. He had tasted it once and it was horrible. He had dipped his finger in Mum's glass when she wasn't looking and sucked it off his finger and it was disgusting. Mum always said that she liked it because it was like a dessert but it wasn't like any dessert Noah liked. It tasted like the worst milkshake ever. Grown-ups like some very strange things.

A couple of hours later, Dad, Noah and Gideon we're wrapped up in their scarves, hats and gloves in the park. Noah was playing in the little house at the top of the slide when he heard a familiar noise.

'Pssst. Up here.'

It was Elmo. He was hidden up in the point of the inside of the roof, his legs and arms pressed out against the sides like some sort of gymnast.

'Hi, Noah. What has happened? Did you come up with a plan?' Elmo asked looking very worried.

'Oh Elmo, I forgot to leave a note. I did come up with a plan. I sent a Christmas Card to the Prime Minister.' Noah replied roll the little elf hidden in the roof. 'I wrote a note in it and explained everything. We just have to hope that she reads it. She'll know what to do.' Noah said, trying to reassure himself as much Elmo.

'Who are you talking to in there, Noah?' asked Dad before sticking his head through the round window on the side of the little house.

'Oh nobody, Dad.' Noah replied sheepishly, 'I'm just playing a game with myself,' he continued, trying hard to not glance up at the elf who was about 30 cm above the bobble of Dad's hat.

'That sounds fun, Professor. We have to go in 2 minutes and get the things Mum needs from the shop. So if there's anything else you want to play on before you go, now is the time.'

'Okay, Dad. Thanks,' Noah smiled as Dad winked and popped his head back outside again.

'Okay, Elmo. I'll leave you a note if anything happens.' Noah said, trying to sound positive.

'We're running out of time, Noah, so I hope it works. I'll be close by if you need me.'

With that Noah slid down the slide and ran over to Dad and Gideon and left the park.

———

In the car, on the way to the shop, Dad put on Christmas FM but there wasn't any music on. Christmas FM was one of those radio stations that played one song and then had 5 minutes of adverts. It just so happened to be one of the advert breaks.

'Christmas is special for all of us, but especially for our children,' a ladies voice said through the radio, 'it's really important that we make sure it's everything they dream of. Toys International Inc. can make sure that any of our excellent plastic toys will be available and delivered before 5 pm on Christmas Eve. That is our guarantee, all for a delivery fee of £10. Nobody on earth can deliver like we can this year. Order through our website.'

'Nobody else on earth?' Dad muttered. ' I think Santa would have something to say about that. Don't you think so, Noah?'

Noah nodded. He didn't want to say anything because the advert had made him panic. What if he hadn't done enough? What if the Prime Minister didn't see his card? What if it was all too late?

He wanted to tell Dad what was happening but for some reason, he didn't think he would believe the story. Like I said, sometimes grown-ups are too distracted by other things and sometimes that means that they just don't believe everything children say. Maybe he would tell Dad later when he worked out what to say but for now, they had to go and get some more things for Mum's party.

When they got home they arrived at a house full of treats. Noah's Mum had cooked enough food to feed 100 people even though there would only be 8 people at the Christmas party; Auntie Sue, Aunt Susie and Esme - Noah's only cousin. Uncle Kevin was also going to be there. I will tell you about them later.

The kitchen table was covered in all sorts of delicious things and Noah couldn't wait to eat them. There were pigs in blankets and Mums speciality, pigs in blankets in blankets which were like normal pigs in blankets but with extra bacon. There were tiny little pancakes with pink salmon on them. There were about 150 chicken strips and 7 different dips. There was also a huge bowl of salad but Noah wouldn't be having any of that. At the other end of the table were cakes and profiteroles and fudge and mince pies and right in the middle was a big round Christmas pudding, Dad's favourite.

'Eeeeeek. It's snowing!' Mum's day could not have gotten any better. She loved Christmas but a snowy Christmas was the jackpot! 'Oh, it's just going to be the best Christmas ever!'

Noah hoped so. If his plan didn't work, it might not be a very good Christmas at all. Oh, he hoped it had worked.

The Doorbell.

 Just after 4 pm Auntie Sue, and Aunt Susie and Esme arrived. Uncle Kevin had a greengrocers shop and was coming round after work, he'd be a bit late. He was always a bit late. Auntie Sue and Aunt Susie were a lot of fun. They always brought fun presents and games and Noah loved it when they visited and in particular when they came for Christmas.

As I said before, Esme was Noah and Gideon's only cousin. Esme was 8 years old and she was the coolest person that Noah had ever met. Some people think that the way to be cool is to wear the right clothes or to have to speak in the right way but those people are wrong. The way to be cool is to be exactly who you are and know that that's the best person to be.

Esme was exactly who she was and that was super cool. The first time that Noah realised that Esme was cool was when she showed him how to do a karate kick. She had been learning karate since she was 4 years old and she was good at it. She was the closest person to a ninja that Noah had ever known, so very cool.

Esme also knew cool facts. She knew so much about astronauts and NASA and space and Noah loved to ask her questions. For his last birthday, Esme had given Noah his Apollo 11 poster and a book about the moon landings. She had told him all about how 50 years ago two men had first walked in the moon.

'I'll go to the moon one day, Noah, if not Mars,' Esme had told him, 'as she was teaching him about gravity. Noah knew she would, she was so smart and cool, she could do anything. One day he hoped he could be as cool as Esme was.

Auntie Sue always brought pass the parcel to the Christmas Eve Eve party. She would write little tasks on notes in between each layer of the parcel and the person who opened it had to do that task. These were always a lot of fun. The music had just stopped on Noah and he was about to do his task which was, 'In the voice of a turkey, sing your favourite Christmas carol whilst standing on one leg and patting your head.'

Noah was just getting to the chorus of Frosty the Snowman and about to lose his balance when the doorbell rang.

'That will be Uncle Kevin,' Mum said, 'I'll go let him in.'

'Where was I?' asked Noah.

'You'd got as far as …' Dad started to say when they heard a great smash of glass from the hallway.

Everyone ran to the hallway to find Mum standing in a puddle of Irish cream surrounded by broken glass. She was pointing at the door with her mouth wide open in a state of shock. Everyone's eyes looked to where she was pointing and discovered that it wasn't Uncle Kevin at all.

'Does Noah Fisher live here?' came a very familiar voice. For stood at the door giant two giant security guards was Eleanor Stiles, The Prime Minister.

'It's, it's, it's y-y-y-ou,' Mum said in a quiet voice. 'It's you. It's Eleanor Stiles. Here. In my driveway.'

There was a long pause. Nobody seemed to know what to do.

'I'm Noah, Prime Minister.' Noah said with a wave, he didn't know why he waved but it seemed right at the time.

'Oh, sorry. Come in, come in,' said Dad suddenly coming to his senses. I'll get you a tea, or a coffee or wine or …'

'Not necessary Mr, Fisher. I am here on very important business and I need to speak to Noah.' Eleanor Stiles said in one of those voices that makes everyone pay attention and do everything they are told.

'Is this about his card? Did he win? Oh, I hoped he'd win' Mum said, still in a very quiet voice.

'Noah, can we sit down and have a little chat about your card please?' The Prime Minister asked stepping inside. The giant security guards closed the door behind her and stayed outside.

'Let's go to the living room,' said Noah, who was the calmest person in the room. His plan had started to work, but he still had to convince the Prime Minister he was telling the truth. 'Follow me.'

Eleanor Stiles glided through the hallway and past the puddle and broken glass and straight into the living room. She looked around the room and then sat down on Dad's favourite chair.

'Nice tree, by the way,' she said nodding towards the Christmas tree. Mum let out a little giggle as if she'd just been tickled.

'Ohhh thank you Prime Minister,' she said but The Prime Minister continued.

'What you wrote in your card if it is true, is a very serious matter indeed, Noah. If what you say has happened really has happened then we need to act fast. Tell me everything you know about this very urgent situation.'

'Yes, I will, but can I go and fetch something so that I get everything right? I need my notebook. Noah ran upstairs to his room and opened the door. He walked inside and there on the bed was Elmo.

'I'm coming downstairs with you, Noah,' he said. 'I think I can help.'

'Umm. If you're sure. We need to go now, come on,' Noah said as he grabbed his little orange notebook and ran downstairs.

When Noah entered the room with Elmo everyone fell silent.

'Is that an elf?' Esme asked, 'this is so cool!'

'Everyone, this is Elmo V Mistletoe, he is one of Santa's elves. He will tell you everything that's been happening. Over to you Elmo,' Noah looked at Elmo and then looked around the room. Everyone else now had their mouths wide open in shock. Even the Prime Minister.

'Tell them, Elmo. Tell them everything,' said Noah.

Elmo told them the whole story. He told them all about Meredith Bleak and her plan to become a bazillionaire (Noah reminded him that wasn't a real number) from selling toys at Christmas. He told them about Santa disappearing from the Grotto. He showed them Nigel Grim's card.

'Our agents are Elf-I-5 are sure that Santa is being held at Toys International's Factory, Prime Minister,' Elmo finished, 'can you help us save him? Can you help us save Christmas?'

'Well. We better get moving. Charlie! Get the car started. Mr Fisher, Noah and Elmo, you better come with us. Mrs Fisher still seems a little shocked by her hero turning up on her doorstep unannounced. One day she would tell this story to her friends and forget to mention dropping her drink. You'll need warm clothes, it's freezing out there.'

'Okay. Okay. Okay,' Dad said, still taking it all in, 'let's get you into your coat, hat and gloves, Noah. I'm sure we won't be too long, Love, and we are in the safest hands of all,' Dad said hugging Mum.

The Journey to Toys International

 Parked outside The Fisher's house was a huge black car. It made Dad's car look like a small car even though, as Dad, always told people, it had the most boot space over every other car in its range. Noah didn't know why boot space was so important to Dad, but it was.

As they approached the car one of the giant security guards opened the door for them and The a Prime Minister, Mr Fisher, Noah and Elmo climbed inside.

'Thanks for coming, Dad. I'm sorry I didn't tell you what was going on. I didn't know what to say,' Noah said holding his Dad's hand.

'Oh don't worry, buddy,' Dad said with a smile, 'Everything is going to be alright, Ms Stiles will know just what to do. She always does.'

Then they were off. The huge black car was much higher up than all the other cars and had so many little lights and gadgets in the dashboard that Noah felt like he was in some kind of spaceship. He couldn't help thinking that Esme would have loved it in this car, she would have been explaining what all the little gadgets did. He would tell her all about it when this was all over.

Eleanor Stiles was on the phone to someone but was talking so quietly that Noah couldn't quite make everything out. The only sentence he heard clearly was, 'and that's when you drop in. Be ready. We have to get this right.' She was so impressive. Noah could see why Mum thought she was the best.

The car raced through the dark, snowy evening for about an hour. The whole time Noah kept looking at Elmo who seemed very worried. He'd clearly been through a lot and out of everyone in the car perhaps this rescue was most important to him.

'It's going to work out, Elmo,' Noah said, trying to encourage the little elf, 'I just know it is.'

Elmo briefly looked at Noah and nodded, 'I hope you're right, Noah. I hope you're right.'

'We are here Ma'am,' came a voice from the front seat.

'Thanks, Richard,' Eleanor Stiles replied in a serious tone. 'Right. This is the plan. I've had the army send me through a map of the factory. We think there is only one place where Meredith Bleak could be holding Santa without any of the workers finding out about her awful plan. We think Santa is in her office. That's on the third floor. There is only one door in and out of the building which is across the courtyard from the main gate. We need to find a way to reach that door and open it without anyone seeing us. Once we've done that two of my bravest soldiers will parachute in and go in and rescue Santa and if things go according to plan, arrest Meredith Bleak. She will not get away with this.'

Noah, Dad and Elmo all stared at the Prime Minister as she spoke. Noah was right, she knew exactly what to do.

'So this is where you come in. Noah and Mr Fisher, you are going to go to the front gate and press the buzzer and start singing Christmas Carols. Say you're there for charity. When the guard comes out and opens the gate, Elmo, you're going to sneak in behind him and hide. You must not, under any circumstances be spotted. Once the guard is distracted by Noah and Mr Fisher's singing you need to race across to the door which is on the left-hand side of the courtyard at the bottom of the tall building and open it.

Once you've done that shine this torch up into the sky and flash of three times,' she handed Elmo a little silver torch, 'three times exactly, no more or no less. That is important. Once you've done that Elmo, find somewhere to hide and wait until we come and get you.

Those three flashes are the signal to my two soldiers will drop out of the sky and head in and complete the rescue. Does everyone know what they have to do?'

All three heads nodded in agreement.

'Good. We are all counting on you,' the Prime Minister said in a way that made Noah (and his Dad) feel like they were in a Hollywood   film.

The Rescue

 At 9:30 pm, which was way past his bedtime, Noah, Elmo and Dad climbed out of the car and made their way towards the gate of the factory. They were all very nervous but all three decided not to let the other two know that they were. Noah could feel his heart racing and, even though it was still snowing, he felt very hot and sweaty under his hat.

The Toys International Inc. factory was a huge building. It was lit up with that orange coloured light that you sometimes see in big cities. There were 5 main buildings and a smaller one at the gate to the whole place. Two of the buildings had giant chimneys that were belching out thick black smoke. The whole place smelled terrible and Noah felt like he needed to cough the closer he got to it.

When they were about 50m away from the gate Noah could see the guard. He was almost as tall as the two security guards that came to his house with the Prime Minister. He had a  bald head and even though it was dark outside he was wearing sunglasses. Noah pointed to the guard.

'That's Nigel Grim,' said Elmo, 'We found his card, remember?'

'He's massive!' Dad said, wondering if this was a good idea.

'Don't worry about him,' said Elmo, 'he looks scarier than he is. How he looks is enough to scare most people. That makes him good at his job.'

With that Elmo darted off into the shadows and hid near to the gate. The plan was about to begin. Noah and his Dad walked slowly up to the gate and pressed a little silver button beside a green light.

Buzz. Buzz. Buzz. Buzz.

It felt like it buzzed forever before there was a voice on the other side.

'Hello?' Who's there?' the voice said. Both Noah and his Dad were shocked for a moment because they could see that the voice was Nigel Grim's, he was speaking into a microphone in the little gatehouse, but

 what they heard didn't suit the giant man at all. His voice sounded more like Gideon's voice than the one you'd expect a scary looking man like Nigel to have.

'Hello? Hello?' he asked again in his squeaky tones.

'Oh hello. Sorry. Hello. We are here singing carols for, umm, for the uh, Captain Christmas's Children's Charity,' Dad said in a very unconvincing voice. Noah almost laughed but managed to hold it in. Even in a serious moment like this, his Dad managed to do something silly.

'Oh good. I love carols. Do you know Frosty the Snowman?' cheeped Nigel, 'I'll come out and sing along with you.'

A few moments later, Dad, Nigel and Noah we're singing a very bad rendition of the song. If you could have been there to see it, you would not have believed your eyes.

Noah kept one eye on Elmo who had sneaked through the open gate and was carefully making his way between parked trucks and huge crates and was getting closer to the door. They were running out of songs and Elmo was only have way to the door.

'Let's sing it again, Dad,' Noah said but before Dad could reply Nigel Grim has started into a very high pitched version of Jingle Bells. Noah and his Dad looked at each other in shock and joined in as best they could, but it was much too high for Dad to sing.

Noah watched as Elmo reached the door but the little elf was struggling to reach the handle. He was stood on his tiptoes but he could only touch the underside of the handle. Elmo jumped and almost got it. He jumped again but missed. The third time he jumped and bingo, he grabbed the handle, his little feet just off the ground. Elmo swung his legs a bit and the handle opened the door cracked open and just in time too.

'a one horse open sleighhhhhhhh!' the three carol singers howled just as the three flashes form the torch shone into the night sky.

From that moment everything happened quickly. Out of the darkness, two soldiers grabbed Nigel Grim and just as quickly as they appeared disappeared with him into the darkness. All that Noah and Dad heard was a little muffled squeak as the huge man was dragged away.

At the same time, two soldiers rushed up the stairs and burst into Meredith Bleak's office and just like they expected there was Santa tied to a chair with a sock in his mouth to keep him quiet. They quickly cut him free.

The whole thing was over in about two minutes. The soldiers appeared with Meredith Bleak in handcuffs. She was a very short woman but with very tall black hair, almost as tall as she was. She stared at Noah as she came out the door, he looked away. Noah wondered why someone who could look at a child with such anger in her eyes would ever want to make toys for children.

Just as Santa walked through the door behind the soldiers to be greeted by Elmo a huge helicopter appeared and landed in the courtyard of the factory. The two soldiers bundled Meredith Bleak into it, saluted to Noah and jumped in themselves. Elmo waved to Noah and followed Santa into the craft and just like that took off into the night sky.

Noah followed the red flashing light on the tail of the helicopter until it vanished. He gripped his Dad's hand tightly.

'Wow. That was fast. It all happened so quickly, Dad,' he said looking up at his Dad's face. Noah's Dad looked down and smiled.

'You saved the day Noah. I am so proud of you!'

A very special person.

Noah didn't remember getting home from the factory. He must have fallen asleep in the huge black car on the journey. He woke up late the next morning in his bed but was still wearing his clothes. He wondered if it was all real at all or had he imagined that he'd rescued Santa the night before.

He got up and went downstairs to find his Mum and Dad having a cup of tea and mince pie with Uncle Kevin and the Prime Minister. Mum had calmed down a lot and she was asking Eleanor Stiles about something called the wage gap, but Noah didn't know what that was. All he knew was that both Mum and Eleanor Stiles were very keen to make sure it didn't keep happening.

Uncle Kevin has the look on his face that everyone else had displayed the night before. His mouth was wide open and he was just staring in disbelief at the fact that Prime Minister was sat in front of him with mince pie crumbs on her suit.

'Oh there's our hero,' the Prime Minister said with a big smile, 'because you paid such great attention and kept your eyes open, Noah, Christmas has been saved.' Noah smiled. He felt proud of himself.

'I came today to give you this,' she continued reaching into her handbag, 'it's a medal for bravery that we usually only give to spies or detectives who have solved a big case. You deserve it as much as any of them, and you're by far the youngest to ever earn it. Congratulations.'

She handed Noah a square, leather box. He

opened it and inside was a round silver medal with the Queen's head on it and a red, white and blue ribbon. He looked up with a big grin on his face to discover that his Mum and Dad were grinning back at him. He even thought that Gideon was smiling too.

'You're going to grow up to be a very special person, Noah,' the Prime Minister said. 'No. I'm sorry, that's not right at all. You're already a very special person. Sometimes us grown ups forget just how special children can be. We really should pay a lot more attention to your ideas. Well done, Noah, we are all so proud of you.'

Eleanor Stiles told the Fishers that Santa had been returned to his workshop and was preparing for the busiest night of his year. Meredith Bleak had been taken to a secret location to be asked a lot of questions about her plans to become a bazillionaire at Santa's expense.

'That's not a real number, Ms Stiles,' Noah interrupted and couldn't understand why all the grownups laughed. Even Uncle Kevin found it funny.

A close call.

Noah, like almost all children, didn't sleep well on Christmas Eve. Most children get very excited about the chance to hear sleigh bells on in the garden or to glimpse a reindeer flying past their window. Not Noah, well not this year anyway. Noah couldn't sleep because no matter how he counted it up, he wasn't sure that the rescue has left Santa enough time to get across the planet to every house. He comforted himself with the idea that Santa was magical and would know how to make things work.

Noah woke up to find his Mum, Dad and Gideon standing at the end of his bed holding stockings.

'Time to get up, buddy.' Dad said, 'you've slept until 10 am. Noah climbed out of bed and the family had a big hug.

'Happy Christmas to my three best boys,' Mum said.

'Happy Christmas Mum,' said Noah squeezing her tightly.

'Let's go down and see what's under the tree,' Dad said, 'Do you want one of Dad's social Christmas hot chocolates, Noah?'

Dad's special Christmas Day hot chocolates were the same as any normal hot chocolate by the way. The only difference was that they were in a Christmas cup. Noah loved them anyway and nodded his head to Dad.

An hour later and the living room of 5 East Green Avenue was covered in wrapping paper. Gideon was playing with his red race car and Dad was trying (and failing) to do a puzzle that Auntie Sue and Aunt Susie had bought him. Noah's Mum was having her first nap of the day on the big chair. This always happened, she used up so much energy being excited about Christmas that by the time Christmas Day came around she slept most of the day.

Noah had received lots of great things this year. He, of course, had got all of the usual things; socks, chocolate, a book, something that needed a type of batteries that Mum and Dad didn't have and a pair of slippers. This year's slippers looked like monster feet with big claws on them. Noah loved them.

Noah's favourite present was a spy kit. It had lots of very cool things in it. It had sunglasses that had little mirrors in them that meant you could see backwards. Now he

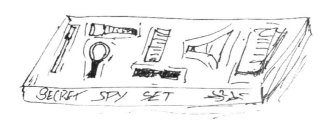

didn't even need eyes on the back of his head. It had a magnifying glass. Dust for finding fingerprints and a book with a hidden compartment in it. It had an invisible ink pen and a special torch that helped you read the invisible messages.

Noah was looking at his spy kit with excitement when he noticed something tucked into the corner of the box. He lifted it out and recognised it immediately as another folded up piece of Christmas paper. It was the exact same kind of paper that was in his advent calendar almost a week ago.

He unfolded the paper expecting it to be another note but it was blank. It must just have been a coincidence. It was strange though. It was folded so neatly and tucked in so precisely. It was obvious someone had out it there.

'I wonder,' Noah said to himself looking at the paper.

He took his special torch and shone it at the paper and instantly a huge grin appeared in his face. The paper wasn't blank at all. As Noah pointed his torch across the page purple letters appeared. This is what it said,

"Noah Fisher,

I can't thank you enough for saving me and for saving Christmas. Without you and your special eye for details, many children around the world would have woken up today and been very sad indeed. If you're reading this note that is all the proof you need that you are a very special person. You have saved Christmas for this year and many more years to come.

Yours sincerely (I don't know which one is right either)

Santa Claus (and Elmo V Mistletoe)"

'What's that Professor Curiosity?' Dad called from across the room.

'Come take a look, Dad,' Noah replied. 'It's really cool.'. He had decided not to keep any more secrets.

Printed in Poland
by Amazon Fulfillment
Poland Sp. z o.o., Wrocław

63820225R00063